Christmas Night Mare

Written and Illustrated
By

Maria Dahlen
&
Sage Stanley

AuthorHouse™ LLC
1663 Liberty Drive
Bloomington, IN 47403
www.authorhouse.com
Phone: 1-800-839-8640

Published by AuthorHouse 07/22/2014

ISBN: 978-1-4969-2752-1 (sc)
978-1-4969-2753-8 (e)

Library of Congress Control Number: 2014913056

authorHOUSE®

Also by Maria Dahlen:

On the Way of the Half Kings

Ode to the Peanut Butter Sandwich

By Maria Dahlen and Sage Stanley:

Night Mare

Coming Soon:

Night Mare - Daymare

DEDICATED TO:

Everyone seemed particularly grumpy that day. It was the last day of school before Christmas break. Mr. B's students had to take one of their teacher's infamous math tests before being allowed to have their class party.

The test was just getting started when a knock came on the classroom door.

Mr. B didn't appreciate interruptions during class time, especially during tests. He made his chair screech loudly in annoyance as he got up to answer the door. His students held their ears in pain.

Mr. B answered the door only to find a strange man with long red dreadlocks, wearing a black leather jacket over what appeared to be pajamas. Next to him stood Sage's mother and Principal Carlson. The students couldn't help but stare as the adults whispered with great animation. They could only guess what was happening.

After a long while, Mr. B finally turned back to his class and called Sage and Tyler to join them.

Glad to be getting out of the math test, Sage quickly got up and wheeled Tyler to the door. Principal Carlson told them that they were being dismissed for the rest of the day and were to go with Mother Mare and Mr. Sand. Mr. B was clearly not pleased. Goodbyes were exchanged and Sandman took over wheeling Tyler's chair briskly down the hall and out of the school building to Mother Mare's van.

"Your tests will be waiting when you return…." Mr. B called after the two children.

"Merry Christmas to you too!" Sage muttered under her breath.

"Sage!" Mother Mare scolded.

It wasn't until they were out in the parking lot that Sage finally asked, "What's going on?"

"First," Sandman warned both children, "Math is very very important! Your teacher had every right to be upset by your leaving. Mother Mare and I would never have pulled you two out of school if it weren't of the utmost necessity." He looked sternly at both Sage and Tyler, wanting to make sure this point sank in before he continued.

Sandman then faced Tyler. "It's going to be you and Mother Mare taking care of the route tonight." Then he turned to Sage, "You and I have something else we need to attend to…." He left things sounding very mysterious.

Sandman hurried everyone into Mother Mare's minivan and they took off for Sandman's headquarters. Sandman couldn't tell Sage this yet, but she was the only one who could save Christmas – to restore the holiday to its true purpose before it disappeared forever. He feared though that telling her this directly might overwhelm her. Failure was not an option.

8

Sandman made sure that Mother Mare's motorcycle was well equipped as he sent Mother Mare and Tyler off on their rounds early that evening. He and Sage needed all the time they could muster to accomplish their mission.

Once the others were off, Sandman and Sage mounted his motorcycle and took off 'the long way around' on their separate mission. Still in the dark, Sage looked back down at the Earth from her side car to see people scurrying around getting ready for Christmas. She saw shopping mall Santas' sitting around with no children on their laps. She saw her friends Kevin and Alex, and her cousin Quinn on the playground discussing there being no such person as Santa Claus, and kicking down a snowman that someone else had just made. She saw stores full of grouchy, ill-mannered shoppers fighting over merchandise, throwing whatever junk they could find into their carts just to give family members they hardly ever saw something of no great importance. It all seemed so fake and meaningless. Christmas always made Sage grouchy. It seemed to make everyone grouchy.

"Is there a Santa Claus?" Sage wondered aloud.

"You of all people should know," Sandman replied.

But Sage wasn't so sure.

Sandman soon pulled into the Pixie Sweets Manufacturing Plant parking lot. The factory was bustling with workers making last minute preparations for the holiday. This was one of their busiest seasons, and no one seemed willing to drop everything to talk to them. Sandman was determined though that they see Blackie, an elf formerly under his employ, no matter how busy he might be. Sandman needed Blackie to turn Sage back into Night Mare.

Spotting Sandman right away, Blackie dropped everything and grabbed his backpack and hurried to meet him.

Miss Kate, the owner, was right behind him, wondering what was up. She saw the small bag of sand that Blackie withdrew from his backpack and was horrified, knowing what the stuff could do. "You still have some of that stuff?" Miss Kate screeched.

Sandman calmed her though, patting her shoulder. "It's an emergency. Please forgive us. Blackie is only trying to help us save Christmas."

Miss Kate stood back then, impressed. She watched as Blackie blew a small cloud of his leftover black sand into Sage's face. Almost instantly she became Night Mare, the large black horse with red eyes that had once haunted people's dreams.

"Come!" Sandman told Night Mare. Leaving his motorcycle in the candy factory parking lot, without another word, Sandman rode the large black mare to the North Pole.

"We're really going to the North Pole? Santa really does exist?" Night Mare asked herself.

Sandman heard her thoughts and answered. "Of course he exists! We've been partnering up every Christmas Eve since forever. Guess who makes sure all of the children have fallen asleep before Santa arrives to deliver the presents? Me!" Sandman proudly told her as he urged Sage, as Night Mare, to push on, faster and faster. They had to reach the North Pole very quickly!

Soon Sandman and Night Mare found Santa in a not exactly jolly mood. He was rushing about the North Pole panicked. They could tell that something was horribly, horribly wrong!

Sandman rushed to his friend and put his hand on his shoulder.

"It's the Christmas magic!" Santa sputtered, "It's almost gone! There's only one reindeer left!" Santa raced to the stables, Sandman and Night Mare close behind, only to see the last of the reindeer, Blitzen, vanish before their eyes.

"What will I do? What will I do? Next it will be the workshop, then the elves, then the presents, and then Christmas itself will disappear! You've got to help me Sandman! Help me! Help me! Help me!" Santa was practically in tears as he grabbed Sandman's jacket and shook him in desperation.

"Don't worry old friend, that's what we're here for. Have your elves hitch up Night Mare and start loading the sleigh."

Santa almost seemed relieved.

"What? Hitch me up?" Night Mare wanted to squawk. She reared up, not liking the sound of this, and tried to get away. How was she, a lone horse, to pull such a heavy looking sleigh, and around the world no less?

But Sandman placed a firm and reassuring hand on her shoulder, "You can do this! You can save Christmas!" he told her.

Night Mare reluctantly submitted to being harnessed, and watched meekly as Santa's sleigh was loaded with millions and millions of toys. "I can't possibly do this!" she told herself over and over again, becoming more and more disheartened. "I can't do this! I just can't do this!"

Halfway through the loading of the presents, Santa's workshop disappeared; the wrapped presents lay scattered in the snow all about the North Pole.

Sandman sighed at this. He shook his head sadly as Santa went into another tizzy. Sage wasn't getting it. Her disbelief was making Christmas disappear at an astonishing rate. "I'd better call in reinforcements," Sandman told himself, and took out his cell phone and placed a call.

Mother Mare and Tyler showed up almost instantly.

"The four of us are going to have to ride along with Santa tonight and do double duty. The magic of Christmas is almost gone, and if Christmas disappears, we're next!" Sandman told his crew.

Mother Mare and Tyler jumped off their motorcycle and began racing around the grounds helping the elves pick up the scattered presents. Sandman and Santa stood off to the side, conferring, while Night Mare continued to sulk and brood as the large sleigh hitched behind her was loaded up.

The remainder of the presents were quickly secured along with Sandman's sleeping sands. Sandman patted Night Mare's side. "It's up to you now. You can do this! We need you!" he told her, getting into Santa's sleigh along with the others.

And with that, Santa's elves vanished.

"Sage! I'm surprised at you!" Mother Mare chastised from the sleigh.

"What? I didn't do anything!" Night Mare snorted irritably.

Tyler got out of Santa's sleigh then and stroked Night Mare's long silky black mane. "It's okay!" he told her.

"Do you believe in Christmas?" Night Mare whispered to Tyler so the others could not hear.

"I do believe in magic! I believe in miracles, in Christmas, and in everything in between! I believe that belief makes anything possible! Believe in yourself Sage like I believe in you!" Tyler patted her muzzle and started back for the sleigh.

Santa stood with the reins in hand, then began to call out the reindeer names – "On Dancer, on Prancer, on Donner, on Vixen…." He remembered himself then, seeing not his beloved reindeer but the large black mare in front of the sleigh instead. He sighed then, "on Night Mare!" Santa half-heartedly sang then and flicked the leader reins.

Night Mare pulled at the sleigh with all of her might, but it wouldn't move. She tried prancing in place to build up enough momentum to pull it forward. Still, it wouldn't move. Finally she bucked and bolted and created a stir to get the sleigh moving, yet it still would not budge.

Santa was up in arms. "It's ruined! Christmas is ruined!" he cried.

But Tyler still had faith. Jumping out of the sleigh, he grabbed a lock of Night Mare's mane and swung himself up onto her back. "The magic's within you! The magic's within you!" Tyler chanted into her ear, growing louder and louder until the others joined in.

Suddenly it felt like a great weight had been lifted from Night Mare's shoulders. They took off like a jet – the horse power of one mighty mare greater than 10-fold that of Santa's nine domestic reindeer.

Up, up, up they went….. The excitement was exhilarating. Night Mare felt giddy with glee.

"Switch on the GPS and present distribution controllers," Santa suddenly told Mother Mare. "Switch on the rocket boosters," Santa told Sandman.

Night Mare came to a jolting halt, almost flipping Tyler off of her back upon hearing this. Suddenly the two found themselves being pulled along by the reins several feet below the rocketing sleigh. "You've got rockets and stuff? Then why was I changed into Night Mare and hooked up in the first place?" Night Mare snorted indignantly. "You don't need me!"

Santa flipped another switch on the dashboard of his sleigh and Night Mare and Tyler found themselves being pulled up into the sleigh by the mare's reins.

Eye to eye now with Night Mare, Santa stroked her mane. "Because my dear Sage, animals are a big part of what makes Christmas magical. With the prospect of losing my reindeer, Sandman thought that you might be able to help." Santa looked at Sandman then. "But perhaps he was wrong…. You aren't really a horse, are you? And you aren't really a young child filled with the wonder and awe of the holiday any longer either…. Perhaps the true magic of the season has indeed been lost to you?" he asked.

At this Tyler jumped down from the black mare and came face to face with Santa. "You're wrong Santa! Sage believes! She's just got to!" Tyler grabbed Mother Mare and Sandman's hands in his then, and they circled Night Mare in their shared belief in her.

And suddenly… Santa disappeared!

In that instant the sleigh jerked to a violent stop. Tyler and Night Mare both found themselves tumbling out of the sleigh — down, down, down.

Sandman was only able to catch hold of Mother Mare's hand to pull her back into the sleigh. Tyler and Night Mare were too far gone.

"Sage! Tyler!" Mother Mare called out desperately, reaching out for them, watching them tumble down, down, down through the clouds.

Sandman had to stop Mother Mare from jumping out of the sleigh after them. "Mother Mare!" Sandman told her firmly but gently, "you have my word that no physical harm will come to them. However I need your help now. It is up to us to deliver all of these presents before all is lost! Help me try and restart these engines…."

Tearfully the two continued on Santa's route. Sandman put folks to sleep while Mother Mare distributed the presents.

And still, Night Mare and Tyler tumbled — down, down, down….

24

When Night Mare finally landed, she was alone. Tyler was nowhere to be found. She cried out for her friend, but there was no reply. She hoped that he was back home and alright.

It was Kevin, Alex, and Quinn who first spotted Night Mare as she stood shivering and alone in the far back corner of the school playground. They had been arguing about Santa not existing when they suddenly stopped, shocked at the sight of the large black horse. Their argument was quickly forgotten.

"Wow! Look at those red eyes!" Alex exclaimed.

"I wonder if that's a giant demon horse that we should vanquish with our swords," Kevin wondered aloud, picking up a twig.

Hearing this, Night Mare grew even more scared, and reared, not knowing if the boys would hurt her.

"That's dumb!" Quinn told them. "Just look at the poor thing; she must be lost," Quinn whispered.

Kevin dropped his twig. "She looks hungry," he added.

"And cold," added Alex.

Quinn went to Night Mare and gently touched her muzzle. The three children led the large black horse through the now quiet playground and into the school building to see Mr. B in their classroom. He would know what to do.

Mr. B had been sitting at his desk, alone in the classroom. He was grading the math test his class had just taken. Hearing the door open he looked up and almost fell out of his chair as three of his students led in a large black horse. The rest of the class quickly filed in, wanting to see what their teacher would do. 'Mr. B,' Night Mare snorted as only a horse could, 'he only cares about math and schoolwork and such. He can't help me!' she thought to herself, her head hanging low in defeat. Mr. B closed his gaping mouth. Quickly picking up the apple that had been lying on his desk, he approached Night Mare. He smiled as he stroked her long black mane and fed her the apple. 'What a magnificent horse!' he thought to himself, mesmerized. "Everyone – we have a situation. We will all need to work together to care for this fine horse."

Night Mare finished the apple and looked at Tyler's desk. Her friend was not there though. She gave a sorrowful cry and shivered. Mr. B looked worried.

"Alex! Kevin!" Mr. B whispered trying to not alarm the horse. "Go to the lost and found racks and bring back all of the warm clothing you can carry." He looked at Quinn then. "Quinn, go to the lunchroom and tell the ladies that we need some fresh carrots for a class project. Ask if they have any to spare."

The three children left the room quickly, glad that they were chosen to help. When Kevin and Alex returned with armloads of clothing, all of the children joyfully covered Night Mare in the coats and jackets, hats and mittens. Night Mare would not eat the carrots Quinn brought though. Instead, she gathered them and laid them atop Tyler's empty desk. A single tear trickled from one of her eyes. 'Tyler would know what to do....' She wished that he were here.

"Sorry girl, but Tyler and Sage were excused early today," Mr. B told her. Night Mare let out another cry. Mr. B stood quiet and thoughtful for a moment. "Quinn, please go and get Principal Carlson."

Principal Carlson was quick to come to the room. He stood at the door, mouth gaping at the sight of a large black horse covered in coats and hats and mittens and such in the middle of the classroom. He called Mr. B over to the door for a quiet conference. Soon, Mr. B was peeking back into the classroom, wide-eyed with wonder all over again. He had been told Sage and Night Mare's secret. Principal Carlson then left him and hurried back to his office to see if he could locate Mother Mare or Sandman via telephone.

"What's going to happen to her over Christmas break?" Peter, a former bully, finally asked Mr. B.

"Good question!" Mr. B replied, eyeing Principal Carlson as he returned to the classroom.

Principal Carlson shook his head no, he hadn't been able to locate either Mother Mare or Sandman.

"I will stay with her. We will go to the school gymnasium and keep occupied until something can be arranged," Mr. B answered.

'Great! He's probably going to try and teach me math.' Night Mare thought to herself.

"I will join you," Principal Carlson added.

"I want to stay too!" Quinn called out, excited. She couldn't imagine being anywhere else.

"Me too!" Kevin and Alex exclaimed in unison.

"Me too! Me too!" came the rest of the class.

No one wanted to leave on Christmas break with something as curious and exciting as a horse wandering about school!

"Then I would suggest everyone line up and go to the office to call your parents for permission," Principal Carlson told the class.

Every single student in Mr. B class lined up. No parent said no. In fact, most parents joined their student as soon as they left work. And soon the gymnasium was filled with students and parents alike – all wondering and worrying about the large black mare.

An impromptu party quickly developed as parents brought cakes and cookies and treats of every sort. Miss Kate and Blackie even caught wind of the party and stopped by to see Night Mare and brought their specialty candy, 'Electric Boogaloo's', to help celebrate.

Despite all of the love and attention and cheer being showered upon her, Night Mare was just as unhappy as ever. 'Christmas is ruined, sleep is ruined, and my being a girl ever again is all ruined!' thought Sage/Night Mare.

Mr. B too was growing more and more concerned. "We'll figure something out Sage," Mr. B whispered to her. "And the math test? I will help you study for it once all of this is all over. You'll do just fine! I know you will!"

Principal Carlson drew Mr. B aside again, as no resolution seemed in sight. "Perhaps we should bring in the 'big guns' and call and see if we can convince Tyler's parents to bring him in. A little Christmas cheer might be exactly what both Night Mare and Tyler need."

Mr. B nodded and went to the office to make this call.

"Mrs. Miller, hello, this is Mr. B, Tyler's teacher. How is Tyler doing this evening?"

Mr. B listened. "Mmhmmm. Seems down? Might be catching something? I'm sorry to hear that Mrs. Miller. I am wondering though, Mrs. Miller, if a trip to school tonight might do Tyler some good. We are having a sort of spontaneous Christmas party here, and have a mysterious visitor in our midst that seems to need some cheering up as well."

After much hemming and hesitation, Tyler's parents agreed to bring him to the party. Within the hour Tyler was bundled up and brought into the gymnasium, accompanied by his parents and little sister.

Night Mare spotted her friend immediately. Perking up, she threw off most of the winter gear that had been piled upon her. Almost tripping over an errant scarf, she dashed across the gymnasium to Tyler. And immediately, and with much relief, she plunked her head down in the boy's lap. Tyler looked visibly relieved as well. Everyone in the gymnasium stood still and stared at the two. 'What's going on here?' everyone seemed to wonder.

"Thank goodness we found one another!" Tyler seemed to tell her as Night Mare nuzzled his cheeks. "Everything should be fine now if you only believe! Believe! Please believe!"

"Believe!"

"Believe!"

"Believe!"

Tyler's voice seemed to chant in Night Mare's head.

And Sage did believe. She had her friend Tyler, she had her school friends around her, and she had her mother. And, she believed that she could indeed pass that math test. Night Mare snickered at this, but she did believe!

Snowmen on the snowy fields
Children on a sleigh.
People shopping and jingle bell
What a wonderful day.

Christmas is coming soon.
Be very good.
If you're bad, be expecting coa
Santa is coming nigh.

Elves wrapping presents.
The reindeer are training.
Santa is getting ready.
At least it isn't raining.

Christmas is coming soon.
Be very good.
If you're bad, be expecting coa
Santa is coming nigh.

Families by the Christmas tree
Children looking out the windo
They're wondering if Santa is re
Most of us already know.

Christmas is coming soon.
Be very good.
If you're bad, be expecting coa
Santa is coming nigh.

The children started singing a Christmas song that they had written to present to their parents….

Christmas Song

Snowmen on the snowy fields.
Children on a sleigh.
People shopping and jingle bells.
What a wonderful day.

Christmas is coming soon.
Be very good.
If you're bad, be expecting coal.
Santa is coming nigh.

Elves wrapping presents.
The reindeer are training.
Santa is getting ready.
At least it isn't raining.

Christmas is coming soon.
Be very good.
If you're bad, be expecting coal.
Santa is coming nigh.

Families by the Christmas tree.
Children looking out the window.
They're wondering if Santa is real.
Most of us already know.

Christmas is coming soon.
Be very good.
If you're bad, be expecting coal.
Santa is coming nigh.

Time in the gymnasium suddenly stood still. Tyler and Night Mare vanished.
Instantly they reappeared next to Santa's sleigh. Sandman had the hood of
the sleigh open and had a monkey wrench in his hand. Mother Mare was
desperately flicking the rocket controls on and off. The sleigh continued to
sputter and spiral and plummet out of control. They hadn't yet been able to
gain control of it.

"Try to get over to the harness. I'll hook you up!" Tyler told Night Mare.
And the two friends made a nose dive toward the sleigh.

Sandman dropped his wrench when he saw the kids, and Mother Mare
visibly breathed a sigh of relief. The two gave each other a high five.
Everything was truly going to be okay now as Night Mare took control of
the sleigh with Tyler on her back as her guide. Sandman picked up his bag
of sleeping sand, and Mother Mare held the first present, as they journeyed
forth to deliver Christmas to the world.

At the end of the night, once all the presents were delivered, Night Mare
landed Santa's sleigh at the North Pole. The North Pole though was still
empty. The workshop was still gone, the deer, the elves, and Santa....
But Sandman assured the kids that everything had indeed turned out okay.
And the two children disappeared then, only to reappear in the school
gymnasium.

The last chorus of the Christmas song was being sung by the school children.

Night Mare lifted her head to see Santa Claus enter the gymnasium.

Putting his finger aside of his nose, eyes twinkling brightly, Santa winked at Night Mare. He had learned that belief goes both ways – that it wasn't only Sage who needed to believe in him, but he also needed to believe in Night Mare as well. Santa stopped in front of Tyler and pulled a beautiful yellow golden retriever puppy from his bag. He looked at Night Mare then with great mischief in his eyes and extracted… a carrot. With a wink Santa then proceeded further into the gymnasium to join the party. He had some more presents to distribute.

'What? Is this a magical carrot or something?' Night Mare protested.

Sandman and Mother Mare were next to enter the gymnasium. They both looked tired but happy; they had completed their tasks of delivering sleep and presents, and were glad to be reunited with the two kids. "I see you two made it okay – thanks to you Sage!" Sandman winked at Mother Mare and fluffed Tyler's blond hair and Night Mare's black mane.

When almost everyone was gathered around Santa Claus, too busy to notice their small group, Blackie went over to the four-some and drew out his wand to change Night Mare back into Sage.

"Whew! Thank you!" Sage told Blackie. She turned and flung her arms around her mother.

Kevin and Alex now raced by with the gifts in hand that Santa had given them. "Bet he's really the janitor!" Kevin told his little brother.

"Yeah!" Alex agreed.

Confused, Sage turned to Sandman. She was curious. "But they don't believe. How come things still worked out?"

"Oh but they do believe!" Sandman replied. "Maybe they don't believe in the person, Santa, but they most definitely believe in the spirit of Christmas – in kindness and giving. It's the feeling of goodwill towards others and the belief in oneself and in others that comes from the heart. That my dear is what Christmas is all about. This wasn't about them, it was about you…."

And the spirit of Christmas filled Sage's heart.

"I must be off. Merry Christmas you three!" Sandman told Mother Mare, Sage, and Tyler, hugging each in turn. "See you all tomorrow." Sandman quickly made his way out the door.

Mother Mare and Tyler's parents exchanged Christmas wishes and left as well. Christmas was alive and well in each and every one of them.

Christmas Haiku

Here comes Santa Claus.

We all believe in him.

We won't get coal.

- Sage Stanley

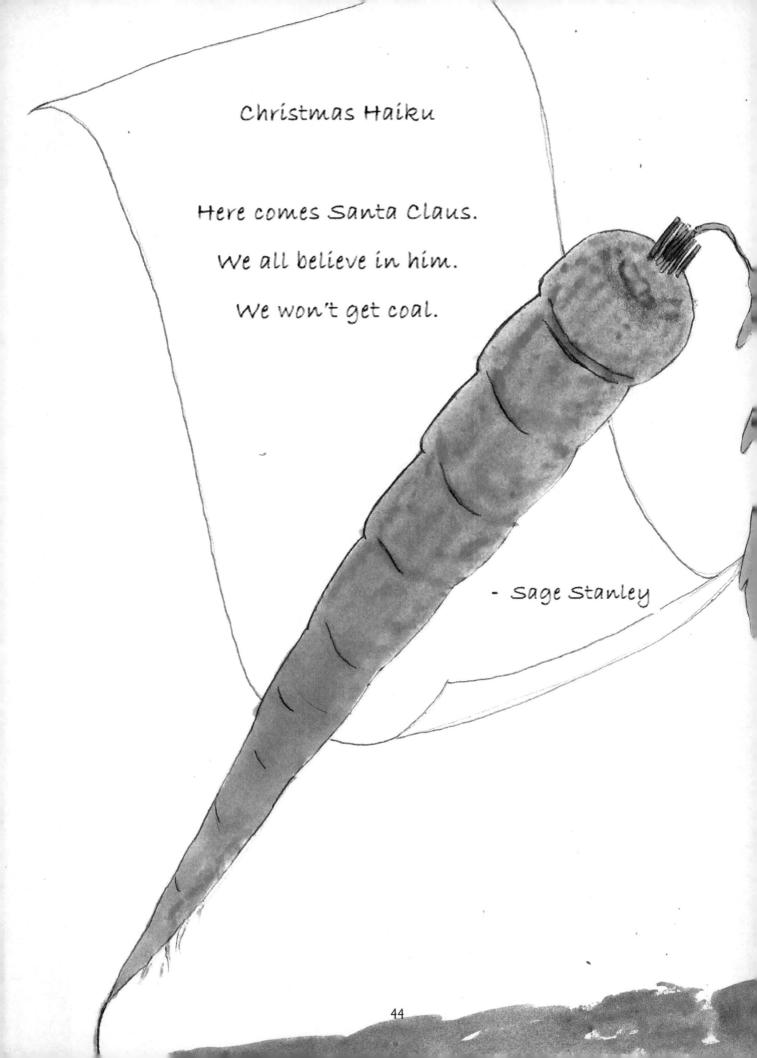

45

CPSIA information can be obtained at www.ICGtesting.com
Printed in the USA
LVOW02s1119080814

398152LV00002B/7/P